To Mary Ann
Forever

IF I HAD A
GORILLA

School Specialty
Children's Publishing

This edition published in the United States of America in 2004 by
Gingham Dog Press
an imprint of School Specialty Children's Publishing,
a member of the School Specialty Family.
8720 Orion Place
Columbus, Ohio 43240-2111

Printed in the United States of America.

1-57768-686-1 (HC)
1-57768-856-2 (PB)

Library of Congress Cataloging-in-Publication Data on file with the publisher.

 2 3 4 5 6 7 8 9 PHXBK 09 08 07 06 05 04

 A Big Tuna Trading Company, LLC/J.R. Sansevere Book

IF I HAD A
GORILLA

Written and illustrated by Mercer Mayer

If I had a gorilla,
I'd take him to school.

Then the big kids
wouldn't pick on me —

if I had a gorilla.

If I had an alligator, I'd feed him fresh fish so he would be my friend.

Then the big kids
wouldn't dunk me
when I went swimming —

if I had an alligator.

If I had a lion, he would
stay with my puppy.

Then the mean dogs
wouldn't pick on him —

if I had a lion.

If I had a snake, I'd put
it in my toybox.

Then my sister wouldn't
mess up my toys —

if I had a snake.

If I had a porcupine, I'd feed
him turnips and take
him to the movies.

Then he could save me
a seat when I went
to get popcorn —

if I had a porcupine.

But I don't have
a porcupine,
a snake,
a lion,
an alligator,
or
a gorilla.

All I have is . . .

a big brother —

and he's almost as good.